mustache, speckle:
loosely to his eyel;
shuts his eyes, and ......

MW01275420

With skillful ease, Morgan glides the weighty log carriage toward the brand-new head-saw. Screeching and tearing, small wood shavings explode skyward and rain down upon his head. He whistles noiselessly, the harmony of his music vanishing amidst the disharmony of the noisy machinery. Usually, Morgan hums and whistles in a subdued and almost vacant manner as he works, but today he puffs his cheeks like a blowfish and zealously blasts out a happy tune.

The crumbled letter from his lovely betrothed, puckers the top pocket of his tattered coveralls. For reassurance, he gently taps it with his fingertips. Minneigan has written to say she would be on the next steamer from Belleoram so they could further plan their Christmas wedding.

Morgan is ecstatic. He deeply inhales the spruce and pine-scented air which is mixed with the mustiness of dampened sawdust, and he feels even more invigorated.

Working alone in the sawmill, Morgan plans to enjoy the day's solitude by breaking in his new equipment and filling one last order before shutting down the mill for the weekend. He enjoys the peace and quiet of working alone, although lately such an occasion rarely occurs. With a dozen men currently employed at the mill and shipyard and with backorders piling up, he'd recently been working sixteen-hour days and has had no time to indulge in the work that brings him the most pleasure—personally converting logs into lumber.

He has promised delivery of this order first thing Monday morning, and it is already Saturday evening. Morgan is cognizant of the fact he possesses an ample share of weaknesses; however, procrastination is not part of that tally.

As he contemplates how his own domestic situation is about to change, Morgan thinks it's time to delegate more responsibility to his younger brother, Wilson. He decides to discuss it with Wilson after church service in the morning and nods his head to signify it's a done deal.

Although the Roberts Brothers' sawmill is quickly becoming a thriving business, it still suffers the growing pains of competitive infancy. Morgan is the majority owner and principal financier of the operation and until now he has been reluctant to delineate his brother's role in the venture. Today, though, Morgan feels compelled to loosen his grip on the reins, a little. He is still mulling over his decision when his thoughts are interrupted by one of his last two departing shipyard employees.

"We's 'eadin' 'ome now Morg. You need anything else 'fore we go?"

"No, byes. Go on 'ome. I'll see you's at church in de marnin." Morgan knows they are anxious for a drop of the town's latest batch of St. Pierre alki and he is quite capable of finishing this job alone. Also, he wants time alone, to think.

"Der's nobody 'ere to 'elp, if you get in a jam," the employees remind him.

"Don't worry, I'll be alright," Morgan said doggedly, dismissing the concerned dual.

Before leaving, though, they load a dozen additional spruce logs onto the log deck.

Morgan begins rolling the logs, one-by-one, onto the carriage. He masterfully glides each log toward the head-saw. Loud screaming sounds nearly rupture his already damaged eardrums as the teeth of the huge saw tear into the logs. In the pit of his stomach, Morgan feels a knot coil tightly. He chalks it up to anticipation. He expects the near week-long wait for the next steamer from Belleoram will be agonizing.

Morgan is smitten with Minneigan, and he realizes she has been his sole motivation to succeed in this business. She dominates his thoughts, day, and night. He could hardly believe it when she said yes to his proposal. He had almost given up hope. But now Minneigan seems just as excited as he, about marriage.

The beginning of their relationship had not gone smoothly.

Morgan recalls his friend's offer to introduce him to the beautiful, educated, charismatic schoolteacher from Belleoram and his initial disappointment when she offered a cool reception to the introduction. While most, who met her, agreed they had been immediately charmed by her warmth and easy manner, she had greeted him with indifference. In fact, when they had first been introduced on a passenger ship headed for the mainland, one might say she had been downright standoffish, brusque even. Regardless Morgan thought of her often as he had roamed around Oregon and California visiting his older sister and working as a travelling salesman.

Inexplicably he had sensed destiny's intent to intervene.

Returning home to his Newfoundland roots two years later he had been thrilled by his good fortune to find Minneigan Cluett standing next to him outside the ship galley of the steamer bound for Harbour Breton.

Morgan frowns slightly, recalling this meeting.

"Good evenin', Mam, my name's Morgan Roberts," he had offered while standing aside to allow her entry to the ship's small galley, expecting she had long forgotten their brief meeting.

"I remember you," she had replied curtly, turning to face him but purposefully withholding her gloved hand. Her penetrating stare had unsettled him, and he had sensed somehow that she read him like an opened book. His confidence had faltered, mindful that there were pages of his young life he would have preferred unread by anyone else, particularly by this beautiful lady.

Much persistence had ensued on that short voyage before she finally began to accept him with the same affinity with which she so readily accepted others. Obviously, she had heard reports of his 'charm,' but her good manners had precluded her from saying as much. During the yearlong pursuit at courtship that followed there were many frustrating moments of uncertainty. But it seemed that each time he despaired, she would make some small gesture or utterance that renewed his determination.

In his quest for Menniegan's affection, Morgan had shunned attempts by family and friends to draw him back into their social circles. His interests had grown surprisingly monogamous.

On a warm blustery evening in early July after many months of courtship, she had finally relinquished to his persistent hints to discuss marriage. Although he had often hinted, he had never actually asked her outright. He had known for some time she harbored an obscure reason to hold him at bay. He had no idea what that reason was, but he had feared she would eventually push him away completely. Finally, she had confided her dark secret to him, which explained not only her reluctance toward marriage but also helped him a little to understand her earlier coolness. Morgan had sighed with relief after her confession and seized the opportunity to propose. Kneeling in the grass where he would later build his home, surrounded by loud rustling of alders and birch, Morgan had asked his beloved Minneigan to become his wife.

And she had readily agreed...

Morgan loads the final log unto the carriage and pulls it forward. Pushing the expelled slab aside, he pulls the carriage back and forth until it yields two-by-twelve planks, ready to be edged and dressed. As he reaches for the saw to make a slight adjustment, a sudden gust of wind, fraught with the smell of sea, forces its way inside the mill, again blasting his face and eyes with sawdust. He lurches forward to sweep the fine dust from his blinded eyes with his left hand and feels a tearing tug on his forearm.

"Goddammit!" Morgan screams aloud and a sickening dread sweeps over him. He immediately realizes he's been cut, but, how badly? Still blinded by sawdust, panic threatens to attack, but he resists. He hits the emergency shut-down lever with his knee just as a burn slowly creeps up his arm, searing his flesh. He raises his hand, but he can't move his fingers. Warm liquid splashes against his face as he wipes the sawdust from his eyes.

Everything is blurred at first. Then he sees the damage more clearly.

Blood sprays against the decelerating saw blade and then spits back in his face. His left hand is missing. Only his thumb remains. He looks at the blood squirting from the remains of his severed appendage and immediately recognizes the extent of his trouble. There is no one within a mile that can help, and he knows how quickly he can bleed to death.

Then the frayed nerves amid torn flesh explode.

In the neighboring community of Deepwater Point, heads turn and brows furrow as Morgan's agonizing screams reverberate across the bay. His bone chilling screams were talked about in that little community for quite some time after.

Meanwhile, Morgan squeezes his injured arm underneath his opposite armpit, and runs. Mindlessly, he bolts over scores of logs, screaming for help as he runs, knowing full well there is none. Passing the employees' store house, he urgently pops the lid off a barrel of flour and drives his injured hand into the barrel hoping to slow the bleeding. He then races across an open meadow before fumbling through a thicket of trees onto a winding pathway. Before collapsing, he runs all the way to Leslie's Meadow, over a mile away.

Mr. Leslie, the telegraph operator, is the only person within a day's journey that has any medical knowledge, whatsoever. And his knowledge is only that which he had acquired years earlier from his father, a purported medic.

Leslie eases Morgan across the kitchen table and scrambles for clean linen to wrap his bloodied stump.

Morgan fumbles with his good hand, extracting the crumbled telegram from his coveralls, soaked with blood, and sweat.

"Tell 'er not to come until she 'ears from me again," he speaks feebly, handing the telegram to the shaken telegraph operator. "Don't tell 'er I'm injured!" he demands before succumbing to the pain and the loss of blood.

Several days pass before Morgan regains consciousness, weeks before he is out of infection's shadow, years before the pain of his terrible loss begins to numb...

Pacing impatiently back and forth the length of planked wharf, Minneigan wills the steamer to dock. The boat is already late, and she feels as if she will burst if she must wait any longer.

Don't come until you hear from me! Morgan's telegram had read. Had he reconsidered his proposal? Why now? Has he changed his mind? Is it just nerves? Those were some of the questions that raced through her mind at first. Now, it's been three days since she received his telegram, and she has received no response to her urgent enquiries. Anger is beginning to infiltrate her anxiety.

Minneigan had heard Morgan Roberts was a bit of a scoundrel before she'd ever met him. But in the years since their first meeting, he had displayed nothing to indicate he was anything but a perfect gentleman, loving and kind. When she'd told him of her dreadful secret, Morgan had held her in his arms and whispered, "My darlin' girl, don't you know that you're the only family I'll ever need."

Minneigan had expected, Morgan, like most men, wanted children and would not be interested in a woman who could not give him a child. She had been prepared for rejection when she told him her doctor had repeatedly warned her that her body could not withstand the stress of childbirth. A childhood illness had left her with a weakened heart that could never be corrected. She had not expected Morgan's overwhelming support when she confessed her torment but was very pleased to receive it.

It was then that Minneigan had enthusiastically agreed to marry him.

Minneigan anxiously awaits the boarding whistle as she watches a group of passengers disembark. She overhears a passenger mention a terrible accident at the Roberts Brothers sawmill. Her heart skips a beat. She tries to remain calm and steps directly in the passenger's path.

"Excuse me sir. I didn't mean to eavesdrop but I'm meeting someone at Robert's Brothers sawmill day after tomorrow and I overhead you mention an accident." She tries to appear casual bur her legs tremble and her heart races uncontrollably.

"Can you tell me what happened?"

"All I know," the gentleman answered nervously, "is that Morg Roberts lost 'is arm at the mill a few days ago."

Minneigan's knees buckle, but the stranger catches her before she falls.

"Is you' alright mam?" He helps her to the gangplank where she clutches the rope railing for support. At first, she's trembling too badly to answer.

Suddenly Minneigan sees a passenger she vaguely recognizes, but remembers that he is from Ship Cove, a neighboring community of Morgan's. She runs toward him, abandoning all attempts to be graceful. The possibility that Morgan had been seriously injured terrifies her.

"Do you have any news from the Head of Bay D'Espoir about a sawmill accident?" Minneigan screams at the startled passenger.

"Yes mam. Der was an accident at Robert's Brothers sawmill." Only a few minutes earlier he had learned of Morgan Robert's gruesome accident from the ship's cook.

"What happened?" Minneigan no longer makes any effort to be polite.

"Morgan Roberts sawed off 'es arm and bleed da death!" the young man replies matter-of-factly.

Minneigan gasps and then screams in anguish, collapsing on the splintered wharf. Blinding pain snakes up her arm and explodes inside her chest. Broken by the tragic news, Minneigan's already weakened heart stops beating...forever.

Morgan wipes away a tear with the stump of his severed hand. Sadly, he shuts his eyes as the schooner that was Minneigan's namesake fades into silhouette and finally vanishes from sight. Understandingly, Sarah, his wife approaches him. Morgan holds her tightly, and as they turn away from the sea to walk toward their home, a shimmering ray of sunlight breaks through the lingering fog bank.

Maine Tornado

Political upheaval, economic turmoil, and ever-changing but never-ending racial tensions, fashioned a caustic environment as the 20th century began its final descent into history.

In Europe, re-unification rallies dominated Germany's social structure, while demonstrators screaming discontent created mayhem in the streets of Moscow. In Asia, China struggled to bury memories of Tiananmen Square as it continued its monumental climb to economic prominence. In South Africa, the black majority celebrated the release of a national hero and authorities demonstrating arbitrary indifference, gunned down citizens in the streets. In the Middle East, Iraq invaded a quiet neighbour, awakening a powerful adversary and igniting a highly televised war.

In North America, though, not even the looming threat of what would become Desert Storm could overshadow the storms of a more routine nature that invaded its countryside in 1990. Many Americans, preoccupied with the blinding snowstorms, which began early in January and persisted throughout the long cold winter months, prayed for an early spring. Then, with spring, came endless torrential rains and devastating floods. However, the most devastating turmoil of all resulted, not from the flooding, but from the tornados that raped the Midwestern states from March to August.

Oddly though, the most unusual and destructive tornado of all was not one in the Midwest but rather one that touched down near the Maine coastline in late August....

A gentle southeasterly breeze, which had blown steadily for days, stopped at mid-morning. The farm-scented air grew close and heavy. Suspended overhead, small cottony clouds spotted the hazy blue sky, creating an illusion that this elaborate creation of nature was actually a colossal still-life painting that spanned the horizon. Glimmering sunbeams reflected off the calm emerald sea, affording a perfect backdrop for this evolving masterpiece of tranquility.

As the morning progressed, this picture of serenity rapidly deteriorated and by noon, Mother Nature's artwork had undergone an ugly metamorphosis. The sky turned menacingly gray and corn stalks danced furiously in the wind. Thousands of birds took flight, further darkening the sky as they swooped toward the rolling hillsides. Thunder rumbled in the distance while overhead a churning cauldron of violent activity heralded the storm's approach.

It was early afternoon when the tornado ripped savagely across the quiet countryside, which bounded Maine's southeastern coastline. The twister's assault was brutal...but the unwary and terrified residents demonstrated a degree of vigilance that would hardly be expected of them, or even, for that matter, of their more experienced mid-western neighbors.

People fled in cars, trucks, tractors, and any type of equipment that was mobile and available. Others had to escape on foot. Every fleeing face exhibited a look of terror that shouted... (Satan, himself, had come to Maine!)

Meanwhile, as local residents distanced themselves from the demon, three less vigilant young students barreled along a dirt road, in an old pickup truck, dodging debris, boldly attempting to catch up to the tornado.

"Hold on tight! Hang on to the side-rail!" the driver shouted as he pealed his pickup truck along the deserted road.

In the back of the vehicle, the other two students struggled to stay upright by pressing their backsides against the cab window and digging their heels into the pitted truck-bed.

"Brace yourselves!" the driver shouted through the howling wind.

"What...?" The woman cupped her ear.

"Like this!" her friend demonstrated, firmly planting his feet far apart and clutching the rusty side-rail with his right hand.

"Oh!" Following his instruction, she woman clutched the rail with her left hand and widened her stance.

"Hang on!" the driver yelled again. "Things are gonna get really interesting now! We've just run out of road!"

When the truck's wheels left the gravel, all hell broke loose. Desperately the young man in the truck bed used one foot to anchor his tripod while he clumsily maneuvered his bulky video camera in place, not daring to let go of the side-rail. Although, jerked around like a kid in a bumper car, the young woman, already, was filming the action with her camcorder. Clearly, the two photographers had great difficulty hanging on to the railing and it was nearly impossible to focus their cameras.

"Oooh shit!" the woman shrieked when they hit a huge mud hole. The recoil tossed her into the air nearly propelling her over the side of the truck and into the cornfield. Luckily, gravity prevailed, and she landed back inside the speeding vehicle, however the camera hanging around her neck snapped upward and struck her squarely between the eyes, splitting the taut flesh of her forehead.

"Oooooh..." she moaned again, rubbing her injured brow. A small trickle of blood snaked along the bridge of her nose and unto her cheeks. "Damn it!" the woman cursed, running her hand across her forehead. The trickle of blood now splattered into her eyes, as it dripped intermittently from the tip of her nose and was picked up by the wind and blown violently back into her face.

"You're bleeding all over the camera!" the young man exclaimed, urgently jerking the camcorder from her.

"Tad, you moron!" she yelled, grabbing for the side rail with both hands. She'd been knocked off balance by her friend's reckless maneuver. Although there was anger in her voice, there was a hint of humor in her eyes.

Tad and Susan had known each other only since the beginning of last semester and except for the past two months had known each other only as a fellow student. A joint research project had recently brought them closer, and a mutual fondness was quickly growing between them. Tad found Susan's quick temper lacked malice but provided a refreshing diversion when many in his new school, in his newly adopted country revered self-control and unnerving social reserve.

"Son-of-a-bitch!" Tad shouted when a clump of cornhusk left an angry welt on his chin and momentarily, blinded him.

"Get down!" he commanded, rubbing dust from his eyes. Grabbing Susan by her arm, Tad flung himself down on top of some tires, and yanked her down with him. "It'll be a hell of a lot safer shooting from this position," he shouted over the roaring wind.

"Not so rough!" Susan pleaded, falling on top of him. "Serves you right," she added while gently brushing the blinding dust from Tad's eyes.

Demonstrating a little more chivalry, Tad gently wiped the blood from her eye with his shirtsleeve. "Susan are you okay?" he asked.

Uncertainly, she merely nodded.

While this drama was unfolding in the back, the driver raced the dilapidated old pickup along a narrow track of farmland that was decidedly better designed for dawdling tractors than speeding automobiles.

Gently shifting Susan aside, Tad rapped loudly on the cab window demanding the driver's attention. Pointing toward an adjacent corn field he shouted to the top of his lungs, "Drive in that direction for about a mile until you pass a yard filled with construction equipment. Then veer right. That should get us back on the road."

Looking at Susan, he added a little more quietly, "hopefully that will also put us behind the tornado and not in front of it."

They were all visibly excited, but also a bit terrified. This was an unexpected development. The three new friends had chased tornados all over the Midwestern States since mid-July, and despite the antiquated equipment commandeered from the audio-visual department, they had managed to shoot some first-class footage. Although incomplete, their coverage was sufficient to ensure additional research funding, provided, of course, they were prepared to embellish the commentary with some colorful narrative. Most of the storms they had tracked were duds and lacked the punch they needed; however, the young students had been fortunate enough to encounter a couple noteworthy twisters.

Their finest shots, prior to reaching Maine, had been taken in the aftermath of a tornado that had ripped through a small Indiana farm community several days earlier. They had missed the tornado, but they had managed to film a little of the life drama that often follows such an event. While they had been filming, a house that had obviously been damaged by the wind, collapsed just as a work crew struggled to get it back on its foundation. The homeowners and their three small children looked on in horror and disbelief...

While witnessing that heart-wrenching sight, the students had experienced an overwhelming sense of helplessness and despair, and they attempted to capture the appropriate footage that would allow them to project those feelings to their audience. Later, they all agreed that the footage of that distraught family would open their presentation on 'Extreme-Weather Conditions.' At least that had been their intention until a few minutes ago.

The three friends had been looking forward to the remainder of summer break and with their research project completed they had been headed back to Nova Scotia when this violence began—*they had certainly not expected today's finale.*

Ironically, only a few hours earlier they had gathered around the kitchen table, enjoying a typical farmer's breakfast while watching the sun peak above the distant hillside and Tad's father had remarked to his son's friends that they could pack away their equipment because they would certainly not see any tornadoes between Maine and Nova Scotia. Now, though, they were chasing the granddaddy of all tornadoes.

Although from their current position, it was difficult to be sure who was chasing and who was being chased.

Tad had arrived home very late the previous evening with his two fellow university students from Canada. They had all been very tired and there had been only a small window of opportunity for fatigued and hurried introductions before crashing for the night. Fortunately, Tad had managed to forewarn his mom and comfortable sleeping arrangements awaited all three.

An early breakfast had afforded the first real opportunity for Tad to acquaint his friends with his parents and vice versa. Tad's father, Peter and mother, Nora had obviously been enthralled with the stories of the young adventurers' summer project but had also been relieved it was over and they made no bones about the fact they thought the trio were more than lucky to get back to Maine unscathed.

"I think you're all nuts, especially you," Peter had chided while offering Susan more homemade toast. "It's scary enough you've been chasing tornados all over the countryside but look at the company you keep," he'd added pointing to Tad and George, who both looked as if they hadn't shaved in a week.

In fact, they probably hadn't.

"Thank you," Susan had added, accepting the offering with a warm smile. "They may look like a bit like wild animals, but I assure you they've been perfect gentlemen."

Tad could clearly see his dad really was bewildered by their tales. He knew his dad could assemble a crane from the ground up with his eyes closed and repair a broken backhoe with nothing more than a safety pin at his disposal, but he knew nothing about predicting weather other than what he could see in the clouds and feel in his bones. Meteorology was about as foreign to him as Nova Scotia had been when Tad had informed him of his intentions to attend Xavier University. Peter had always assumed that Tad would become an engineer, like him. However, he had always taught Tad the importance of making one's own decisions; therefore, he had quickly come to grips with his son's decision and supported him.

Susan had been a big hit with Tad's mom, Nora; their driver, George not so much so. Tad figured his mom had taken an instant liking to Susan during their brief meeting the evening before and donned her match-making cap in the morning. Thus, she perceived George as a rival for her son.

Tad still wasn't exactly certain of his feelings about Susan, but he understood his mom's instant attraction. Susan was impossible to resist. True to her Newfoundland upbringing, Susan had called his mom and dad "My love" when she'd addressed them and patted their hands frequently during breakfast conversation. She'd radiated such warmth toward his parents that she'd effortlessly dispelled any possibility her words and actions could be misconstrued as condescension instead of genuine affection. It was impossible not to succumb to her charm.

"Where the Hell is your construction equipment?" George shouted through the sliding window, jolting Tad back to the moment.

Tad raised his head and looked around, suddenly shocked by what he saw, or more precisely, what he didn't see.

Tad had lived his entire life in this community, and he knew it like the back of his hand. Zork Equipment was the largest sales, service, and rental operation for heavy construction equipment in Maine. And it had vanished into thin air. Not only was there no equipment visible, but also the 250,000 square foot warehouse and sales office was nowhere to be seen. In its place was a massive field of mud and debris. The adjacent office building of his father's employer, Zork Oil and Exploration had also vanished.

Tad's immediate thought was of his father's co-workers, particularly his twin sister, Tracy, who was assisting Zork plan for their father's upcoming retirement. Then he remembered it was Sunday.

Tad breathed a sigh of relief. No one would be there on Sunday.

"Have you ever seen anything like this?" George shouted from his cab.

"Never!" Susan replied without interrupting her filming.

Abruptly the tornado changed direction and raced toward them. It ripped trees from their roots, sucked up the water from a nearby pond, and tore crops out of the ground, leaving only chaos in its wake and it was still showing no signs of weakening.

Both Tad and Susan bounded to their feet in one fluid motion.

"Get the hell out of here!" Susan screamed, banging sharply on the truck cab to capture the driver's attention.

"Quickly man!" Tad shouted, also striking the cab, repeatedly.

"Yeh! Yeh! I see it!" the driver yelled back at them. "Hang on!"

George swerved the truck to the right, away from the approaching tornado, making a mad dash toward a narrow track of fallow farmland.

"Enough is enough! We're out of here," George screamed as he raced away from the storm.

"Yes! Yes! Just go! Drive!" Tad and Susan prompted, settling back on their haunches.

An explosion of lightening suddenly spilt the sky and the tornado simply vanished leaving only an enormous bubble of floating debris which gently settled to the earth. They could clearly see that the tornado had dredged a zigzag pattern across the flat countryside and had left a trail of destruction almost a kilometer wide and as far as the eye could see.

Later, heading back toward his parents' home, Tad contemplated the unexpected developments of this most unusual day but was blissfully unaware of the impact this day would have on him personally or of its importance in general.

The twenty minutes of footage these three young students filmed that morning immediately make headline news in Maine and Nova Scotia and would one day early in the new millennium become vital to the United States Department of Homeland Security.

However, the personal devastation for Tad only became apparent after they crested the hill overlooking his family home. Where the house had stood only a short time earlier, there now remained only an ugly scattering of debris. Where the farm had been there was now a gigantic trench of muck, a kilometer wide, extending to the horizon. Nora was found later that evening more than a kilometer from their home, still strapped into her seat and wedged between two boulders atop an outcrop overlooking the ocean. Tad's father was never found.

A Miscalculation

A gigantic swell mushrooms up from the shimmering black sea. The ballooning wave amasses great pools of frigid water that steadily billow up to the surface from the bowels of the Atlantic Ocean, spawning an oceanic wall of terror; a towering wall of seawater that contravenes the laws of physics. West of this watery divide, sunny cerulean tranquility resides, while east of it, sheer pandemonium takes up residence. A maelstrom of swirling ocean spray, bubbling sea foam, and floating debris, whipped about by gale-force winds, rapidly transforms the eastern sector into a virtual war zone. Defying logic as well as physics, this preternatural wave appears to hover, indecisively, before finally, surging toward the western horizon.

Directly in the giant wave's thundering path, a nebulous apparition mystically appears out of nothingness. This spectral anomaly, shrouded in a peculiar green mist, pitches violently, spitting lightning bolts at the encroaching wave, challenging its attack. Although this mist cloaked object appears intangible, it is seized by the surge and effortlessly catapulted upward, onto the rogue wave's crest where it glows effervescent against the cloudless blue sky. Slowly the mist dissipates and the object that is its core crystallizes, transforming shapelessness into a small, elongated submarine-like craft.

Slowly, this small craft's vaporous shell vanishes, and the lightning abates. As inexplicably as it had arisen, the rogue wave collapses, melting into the ocean, cradling the small vessel into its fold.

An eerie silence signals the angry ocean's puzzling retreat and the waters calm. The tiny vessel's violent jerking motions slowly subside.

Inside the sea craft, in absolute darkness, a lone passenger struggles, cursing under his breath when the harness trapping him into his seat tightens painfully around his abdomen. He twists his body from side-to-side but instead of releasing its hold, the harness draws tighter, causing him to grimace in agony.

He immediately ceases struggling.

His pupils are fully dilated, maybe from the pain, possibly from the assault of utter darkness, but most likely from the gut-wrenching fall as the wave collapses…

…I awaken with a jolt, feeling as if I had been riding the world's highest roller coaster and had just taken the ultimate thrill-seekers plunge while simultaneously being crushed. But this crushing sensation quickly diminishes, and the bizarre fall ends with no noticeable injuries.

But where the Hell am I?

Still struggling with this question, I'm suddenly struck with an overwhelming sense of déjà-vu, and I think, this can't be happening again.

But that's crazy!

Really! Has this ever happened to me before?

The fact of the matter is, I have no idea where I am, nor what exactly has just happened.

My last clear memory: I'm walking along a brightly lit street, in the pelting rain, dolefully wishing I had brought an umbrella, or at least, a cap. After that, I remember nothing, until just now as my chilling roller coaster ride ends, leaving me baffled. It feels like I'm inside a stifling, lightless tomb.

A sudden bout of claustrophobia jolts me and for a moment and I can't breathe. I gasp sharply and then slowly release my breath. I inhale again, slowly, forcing my mind back to my earlier walk in the rain, my last grounded recollection. This helps a little. I breathe deeply and slowly a few times. This also helps stifle my panic.

I also struggle with the worst case of dry-mouth imaginable. I feel as if I'm hung-over, although I know I'm not; I haven't had a drink in years. But I remember the experience well and it was very similar to what I'm now feeling.

This entire ordeal feels surreal, yet jarringly familiar.

This can't possibly be real! I simply mustn't be awake. I must be dreaming.

I shake my head, attempting to clear away the confusion but it doesn't help in the least. My head feels as if it's filled with cobwebs and I truly can't reconcile what I think is real with my current predicament. A gnawing sense of déjà-vu really has latched on to roost and the more I think this dilemma is a dream, stronger grows the impression that I've been here before and that I'm reliving some past experience.

I must remain rational and try to separate fact from fiction.

Attempting to find clues in the utter blackness which surrounds me, I try raising my hands only to find that my hands are also bound, restricting movement to mere finger wiggling.

Water is pounding against whatever it is that's confining me...of this, I'm certain. Waves are crashing all around me; I'm pitching and rolling helplessly, restrained by invisible bonds. Undoubtable I'm trapped in some sort of boat, but how did I get here? I'm reeling in confusion, engulfed in darkness, nearly suffocated by the upper body harness and... I'm terrified. I feel as if I'm being lulled deeper and deeper into a living nightmare and time has become distorted.

I fear I'm losing my mind.

I try harder to regroup my thoughts, but I'm finding it very difficult to focus.

I'm soaked, from head-to-toe with perspiration. Something, silky and wet, stuck to my face, is tickling my nose, adding just a little more discomfort to an already unendurable situation. I can't free my hands to scratch the itch, so I shake my head aggressively attempting to dislodge the annoying assailant. Dampness trickling down my neck makes me wish I had gotten a haircut. I grin at my absurdity, thinking long hair is surely the least of my worries at this moment.

I believe, or at least I hope, I'm dreaming, but I can't find my way back to awake.

I wish I could see something, anything.

Suddenly, as if in response to my silent wish, I'm granted a small reprieve. Electrical static briefly shatters the darkness, and for a few seconds, the world glows florescent green. During this brief period of illumination, I see an obscure image hovering above me. It's a woman whose face I know I should recognize, yet I don't remember. She raises her hand in greeting…or warning…or anger.

The image is hazy and I'm quickly fading. I'm drifting, floating and I'm about to float into oblivion, my mind wandering, my head nodding, my eyes closing, my thoughts rummaging, when, for a split second I see her face, clearly, in the darkness. In that instant, I know with absolute certainty that she is the reason I'm here and briefly I'm warily confident that everything is proceeding as expected. Everything is as it should be and I merely need to remember, and all will be right.

This thought revives me somewhat, but I still can't stay awake for long, and this worries me because drowsiness is certainly not my normal reaction to stressful situations. In fact, quite the opposite is true…or is it?

Really, can I be certain of anything?

It must be drugs, I think, anesthetics, surely.

Although the thought that I've been drugged should worry me, it doesn't. It reassures me. Surely, the side-effects will wear off quickly. Finding comfort in what might well be misplaced optimism, fear releases its grip and sleep grapples to replace it.

Then a loud thump awakens me and a hard, heavy object that is suddenly crushing both my feet, garners my full attention. I try, unsuccessfully to move my feet from underneath the object but restraints prevent me from doing so. As my hands are also restrained, I quit trying to remove the annoying object and reluctantly accept this new discomfort. Maybe it'll help me stay awake, I decide.

It didn't, though.

I don't know how long I'd slept. In this darkness, and in in this stupor, with no point of reference, I can't tell what's real and what's not. Time really does seem distorted.

Regardless of how long I may have slept, I am not rested. Rather I'm feeling an overwhelming sense of dread, and my thoughts are filled with premonitions of doom.

Nothing makes sense and I can't connect my thoughts.

I sense there's great urgency in what needs to be done or there's grave danger...or at least immeasurable disappointment...waiting for me. I struggle for further insight but with my mind wavering to and fro, my efforts are futile. I know I've travelled a long distance for an important reason, but what? Questions are exploding into my mind in an endless steam, but answers remain indubitably elusive.

I truly believe I've been drugged but with what kind of drug? Whatever it is, it's in no hurry to vacate my brain.

I'm still trying to will away the cobwebs when a burning desire to act, to move, to do something, abruptly rages inside me. I instinctively twist and pull against the restraints. But I still can't escape my bonds. I have no idea what it is I feel compelled do but I'm certain I must lose these restraints if I'm to succeed.

Again, I feel my mind slipping and a slideshow materializes inside my jumbled brain: a steady parade of mages that is fleeting, desultory and a little frightening. Frightening, mostly because of my inability to control the steady cavalcade of meaningless images, and because I know they're vital, but I just can't link them. I suppose I'm remembering some things from my own vague past and I'm certain the images are relevant, but presently they mean nothing to me. Some portray blissfully peaceful settings while others depict death and destruction. If this is, in fact, a slideshow, someone has done a poor job of categorizing it into any meaningful order.

A beautiful young woman, sitting with a group of young adults, is sleeping…children playing in a field, chase each other…an elderly couple, holding hands, laugh…a raging tornado, leaves destruction in its path…a woman, whose face is hidden, appears to be dying…a little girl staring with brown-eyed wonder, smiles…a building explodes…an old man in a tattered lab coat holds a smoking pistol…a plane crashes…a woman with tangled and wind-swept hair fumbles about in a forest, dazed…There are many more, but these are just a few of the disconnected images searing my brain.

Wait! The young woman isn't asleep; her head is lowered because she's reading. She raises her head and smiles. Her shoulder-length brown hair hangs softly against her cheeks. She's now sitting at a desk holding a child's book. Other books surround her; however, I recognize the book she's holding because I'd watched her read from it many times. I can't recall who she is but I know she's integral to my predicament.

Her beauty captivates me, her smile hypnotizes me, and her emerald eyes mesmerize me. Am I repressing memories of this remarkable woman? Why in the world would I do that?

Her smile also reignites my desire to act. But what the hell am I supposed to do?

I simply don't know.

More images intrude upon me, but the woman's face remains locked inside my head. I realize, demurely that she's watching me watching her. Trapped and lost, with no recollection of her identity…or my identity…I feel a flash of heat spread upward from my neck, flushing my face. Fighting panic, immersed in cognitive limbo, I'm mortified that my overriding emotion at this moment is juvenile embarrassment…caught, staring for Heaven's sake!

With my thoughts alternating between fantasy and some semblance of reality, I continue struggling with my restraints, slowly gaining a little added mobility. My mind however remains locked onto the random slideshow.

The playing children revisit, but they now appear to be at a distance. Instinctively, I squint my eyes trying to see the children more clearly, forgetting for an instant they are only images in my head. The boys look like twins. They're not though. Sean is two years older than Chad.

Strange! I can't even remember my own name, yet I remember the names of these two boys inside my head, along with their ages and many intimate details of their lives, from cut fingers to college graduations. Obviously, they're my sons but the very thought that I'm not certain of this fact is more frightening than imaginable.

I'm still reeling with uncertainty when the slideshow advances, and the woman is back; this time she's older. Her hair dances gently in the wind and briefly her fragrance transcends the gap between my world of obscure memories and my very real physical prison. I can feel her hair flutter against my face. My anxiety subsides a little, but so again does my wakefulness.

What the hell? Lightning from above jolts me back from slumber. A hissing sound is immediately followed by peripheral motion. Settling back in my seat, I'm able to watch as the sea craft's ceiling slowly retracts in all directions, revealing an overhead portal. Abruptly, a violent torrent of flashing green lights invades my small space and darkness is splintered like broken glass. Green quickly turns golden, and I feel as if hot cinders are scorching my eyes. I'm momentarily blinded. I realize, of course, it's the sun, the glorious and applauded sun, as the searing brightness yields to a gentler shimmering glow. I breathe a sigh of relief, my first since this whole ordeal began. Straining against the hard seat, I see that only a glass or transparent plastic shield remains as a barrier to my freedom, and a wave of relief swells inside me.

The sun is almost directly overhead and for a moment I'm awestruck at its resplendent radiance against the deep-blue sky. I haven't seen the sun unobstructed this way in many years. How is it possible such magnificence could be overshadowed by mankind's struggle for survival?

Huh! My head had seemed to be clearing a little and I felt a little less confused after the introduction of sunlight to my little prison but now…where the Hell did that senseless revelation spring from? Memories are gradually returning but they aren't rational, or certainly aren't making any sense, although something, on the outskirts of my consciences, screams familiarity.

Now that my eyes have adjusted to the gift of sunlight, I examine my surrounding closely and I see that I'm trapped inside an oval chamber that is astonishingly space-age in appearance. Everything from the console, the single seat, and the floor, walls and roof appear to have been carved out of a single block of opaque plastic that omits a silvery gleam wherever the sunlight touches. Even more spectacularly, I'm clothed the same as my surroundings. Bathed in the sun's rays, I look as if I've been tightly wrapped in aluminum foil, shiny side out.

More extraordinary, still, is the fact that this entire scene stirs me to nostalgia, instead of incredulity. It's like watching an old movie with my children while wistfully recalling the times as a child when my siblings and I huddled around a small black and white TV, watching the same movie. I remember both scenarios vividly and the Wizard of Oz springs to mind. I smile, thinking, if they had had the outfit I'm wearing when that movie was made, instead of the clumsy stove-pipe costume, which first nearly castrated and next nearly asphyxiated Buddy Ebsen, during filming, he may have become better known as the Tin Man rather than as Jed Clampett of the Beverly Hillbillies.

My life is returning in disjointed bits and pieces and as I shrug away my melancholy ghosts, I'm surprised that my fleeting reminiscence of childhood which has imbued me with optimism, encouragement, and downright elation, has also made me feel more grounded in reality than is warranted. I guess when you've lost practically all your memories even the slightest recall can be is monumental. Regardless of the explanation, I am comforted by my ephemeral detour down memory lane.

Whining, mechanical resonance, followed by more hissing sounds of compressed air being released, alerts me to some new developments occurring. Then suddenly, as if they had never existed, the bindings immobilizing my arms, legs, and abdomen, vanish, blending impossibly with—no! actually melding into the seat. I push aside the large plastic block which is barely discernable from the vessel's interior and which I've discovered is the culprit that has been crushing my feet. I stretch my legs and rub my wrists and for the first time I notice I'm wearing an odd looking wristwatch. The blank face is shiny and black and is encircled by a pasty band with many unusual markings on its edge, a dial of some sort. I raise my arm into the sunlight and the watch gleams silver in the sunlight.

Everything around me is similarly constructed.

I nimbly touch the watch face and 2020.07.30 appears, and then disappears again. Next 08:22:21…explodes across the tiny screen.

That can't be right!

I look up at the sun, which is almost directly overhead, only having slipped ever so slightly toward the starboard side of the portal. I stand and press my face against the glass to get a better view of the horizon and for a moment I'm shocked that I'm surrounded by water; calm, black, ocean, extending to the sky in every direction.

There's been a mistake!

I'm enclosed inside a mini submarine, but for some reason I'm not surprised about this, as if it's normal, expected even. But for reasons unknown, I'm astounded there's no land in sight. Something feels wrong.

I try to suppress a growing premonition of doom and concentrate on determining the nature of error I'm sensing.

Logic tells me it's early afternoon, but I'm not certain how much I should rely on my judgement today. I tap the watch with my fingertip and give it a quick shake.

08:19:15.

The time display indicates it's several minutes earlier than the last time I checked. Impossible! Obviously, it's not displaying time. It's counting backwards. It's not a watch; it's counting down!

Suddenly I remember exactly what it is, its purpose anyway. Actually, remember isn't quiet the correct term, more imprint than memory, no preamble, no drum-roll; recognition is suddenly just there on the tip of my brain. I have a working knowledge of this little electronic device although I have no recollection of seeing one before and I have no memory of previously using it. It's a remote control required to operate my vessel and the timer has been preset to coincide with the completion of my abstract mission. I know this as surely as I know my name.

Only, I don't know my name!

More mechanical whining noises resonate from below my seat while an abrupt sinking sensation hints added trouble is brewing. As the sun's brilliance fades rapidly into watery distortions, I am horrified to discover that I really am sinking; a realization that propels me to full alertness.

Slowly, the overhead portal, my window to the skies, my last barrier to freedom, slides forward. Ice-cold water gushes inside my chamber, crashing violently against by head and chest, compressing me against the seat, forcing the air out of my lungs. Ironically as I'm gasping for air, I remember who I am, my name anyway. My most significant memory recovery. Yet, I can't rejoice because my immediate peril is drowning and thoughts of escape are suddenly paramount.

The portal has only partially opened and has ceased moving. I quickly estimate that the exit is too small for me to squeeze through.

Fighting against the barrage of seawater, I desperately fumble with the overhead hatch, but it refuses to budge. Pulling, tugging, clawing, hammering with my fist, all prove futile as the glass portal stubbornly refuses to either shatter or open fully.

Panic threatens my struggle for self-control and my mind is reeling.

I'm drowning! No! Don't panic! Panic kills.

Recognizing my father's warning from another lifetime that is resonating inside my head, I begin to calm. But it's a frightful battle.

I must think my way out of this. I know the wristwatch device controls the vessel but I'm trembling violently, and my fingers can't manipulate the tiny controls no matter how hard I try. I breathe deeply just as my chamber is filled with water and I hold my breath dearly, knowing it may be my last. I can't see what's preventing the portal from opening all the way and I'm now sinking rapidly. Fortunately, pressure equalization prevents further assault from crushing water so I'm free to move. I float upward hitting my head against the portal and when I do, I feel an abrupt jolt. The overhead door rapidly closes and then springs wide open.

Mercifully, I'm freed.

I glance down as I exit the vessel and I read the name "Reunion" sprawled across the top of the vessel and oddly, especially under these circumstances, the name stirs pacifying though vague feelings of security.

I release some of the air from my lungs and follow the air bubbles upward. As soon as my head breaks the surface, I deeply inhale the salty air and nearly choke on the cold, salt water that I managed to not swallow on my way up. I take another breath, savoring the moment as a bone crunching tremor reverberates through my entire body. My fleeting moment of bliss abruptly ends. I realize how little time I have before hypothermia sets in. I look around in every direction, confirming what I already know. "Oh no! I'm in big trouble."

Almost immediately though, I can feel the heat from the sun and even though the water is frigid, my entire body soon begins to tingle with warmth. My trembling subsides. This might be the onset of hypothermia; I despairingly consider this is very likely but then I realize the suit I'm wearing is heating my body. The silvery gleam of my clothing has transmuted into golden luminosity, and I can feel waves of heat radiating from it. As fantastical as this seems, I know for certain this is also normal and I should have expected it.

I quickly discover that, in addition to the life-saving heat, my clothing also is providing buoyancy.

This is very fortunate. I'm certain now that my predicament has been anticipated and hopefully someone has likewise prepared for other contingencies.

Now, though, my most pressing problem is finding land but before I can do that, I must establish my location. My eyes drawn to one particular direction; I quickly scan the western horizon. I am greeted with an endless expanse of white-crested charcoal sea, and I feel a gentle breeze against the back of my head.

Though it's not noted for its gentle breezes, I believe this is probably the North Atlantic, but I can't really corroborate my reasoning.

It's simply another imprint.

If this is the North Atlantic Ocean, a breeze can whip up a gale quickly, I think, and this concerns me immensely. The idea of swimming enters my mind, but I immediately dismiss this option as ridiculous since I can see for several kilometers in every direction and there's no outline on either horizon to suggest land is anywhere nearby and definitely not within swimming distance. This doesn't worry me as much as it should though; another memory-imprint tells me I have options.

I study the ocean depths, searching the darkness until I spot a sparkle of light radiating from beneath the water, several meters to the west of my position. Swimming the short distance quickly, I spot the outline of a large mass directly below. It's just as I suspected, the sea-craft I'd arrived in, now hovered only a few meters below the surface. I'd initially assumed it had gone to the ocean bottom after my evacuation. I now realize that "Reunion" hadn't sunk after all; it had been programmed to descend and remain under the water until required.

Why?

The answer to that question eludes me, but I know what I must do next.

I reach for my watch and slowly turn the peripheral dial, clockwise. The tiny monitor script changes from... 08:15:09... and scrolls through various options.

...warning...velocity...transfer sequence...messages...

I stop, and then turn the dial counterclockwise. The script immediately reverses until the timer displays 08:15:01. I continue turning the dial counterclockwise and the monitor display again scrolls through options.

...*climate control...depth...direction...*

"Depth!" This is the function I need, the one to activate the vertical positioning controls which will permit me to float Reunion to the surface again. I lightly tap the watch and 3.1 meters blazes across the center of the small screen: above and below the script are arrows pointing up and down. I touch the up arrow and immediately I feel the ocean agitate beneath my feet. The depth reading slowly decreases as I monitor Reunion's slow ascent to the surface.

Anxious to assume my search for land, time seems endless while waiting as my ride continues its tedious ascent. As soon as Reunion nudges my feet, I feel around underneath the dark ocean, searching for the open portal. When I finally find the opening, I maneuver my feet and legs inside the chamber, positioning myself for easy access after the vessel fully emerges above the ocean surface. Soon I begin to rise with Reunion and when its short journey has finally ended, I'm sitting on top of a most unusual sea-craft, two meters above the gently rolling waves with my legs dangling inside the flooded chamber. My outfit is still radiating heat waves to my legs and midsection and emits a golden glow while my arms are gleaming with silver in the sunlight. I touch my face and discover the suit covers me entirely. I must be a sight to behold!

Climbing to my feet, I stand upright to survey my surrounding from new heights; Reunion's apex is two meters above the ocean surface and I'm just under two meters tall. The added height extends the horizon many additional kilometers, but distressingly, there's still no land in sight. Land should be to the west. That is, assuming my gut feeling is correct, and I am, in fact, somewhere off the east coast of North America. At this moment, though, I'm wary about any underlying motives I might have for formulating this assumption. Land could just as easily be east of my position.

Straining my eyes while shielding them from the glare with by hand, the bright sun on the pulsating ocean blinds me. Slowly adjusting to the brightness, I still see only sparkling and twinkling of whitecaps dancing atop the boundless ocean.

I notice, though, that I need not have worried about gaining access to the portal from the water, since ladders were carved into both sides of the vessel, extending from the water line to Reunion's portal. I again notice its name etched into the flawless hull and once more, it sooths me.

I detect motors churning beneath my feet and nearly imperceptible sounds trickle up through the open portal. Clicking and swooshing, swooshing and clicking. The portal suddenly closes and the air around me explodes into multi-colored droplets as dozens of water jets erupt from Reunion's hull. Within seconds, Reunion's inner chamber is water-free. The portal opens, slowly. I adeptly lower myself inside. I know just where to place my hands and feet for easy entry. It's obviously not the first time I've entered through this small portal, but I still can't remember when.

I glance at my wrist monitor 08:01:17. The countdown has nearly reached the eight-hour mark. But what is the significance of this countdown? Eight hours for what?

Thirty minutes has already elapsed, and I still have no idea why I'm here or even where I am but I have a strong feeling that every minute is vital.

Messages...?

It suddenly occurs to me that one of the panel settings had read...messages.

"I wonder?" I toy with the monitor...*messages* appear on the tiny screen. I press gently with my thumb and a message immediately scrolls across the tiny monitor. ...*You may experience amnesia. Don't enter the harbor until you know why you're there.* A short and sweet command, but reassuring nonetheless, as someone, at least, had been prepared for my amnesia.

Harbor? What harbor? I still don't know if I can even find land! If there is supposed to be a harbor visible, someone has seriously miscalculated my coordinates.

"Well, let's see if I can find a harbor," I try to vocalize but only garbled whispers escape my constricted throat. I swallow painfully and again try manipulating my wristwatch. I find a setting...*Guidance Positioning...* and verify my instinct for direction had been correct; however, I'm almost one hundred kilometers from Newfoundland, the nearest landmass. I open the sequence for ...*speed...* and the craft's quiet motor immediately responds. A few seconds later, I'm cutting through the water at nearly thirty knots. There is nothing more I can do but travel in the direction I've chosen and hope for the best.

I slump into my seat, rest my head, and expel a long sigh. The steady roar of engines along with the rhythmic beat of water lapping against Reunion's hull soon relaxes me. My eyes are drawn to the large block of plastic that had earlier caused me such discomfort and I reach out to retrieve it. It is very heavy and is about a meter long and almost half that again in width and depth. I raise it unto my lap for closer examination and find that it's a solid block of opaque plastic which blends exactly with its surroundings. It has no creases, lines, or blemishes whatsoever. But as I turn it on my lap a digital display of zeros appears on one of its flawless faces; six zeros in all. My memory is slowly returning. I check the time setting on my watch and note 07.57.49. Again, I'm overwhelmed with a sense there's been a tragic error, however I turn the watch face to *...transfer sequence...*, touch it gently and the same digits appear on the plastic block's digital display. Immediately a line forms around the center of the unusual object and its top and bottom portions separate.

Inside the top portion of the unusual container, I find a black sweatshirt, a black hoodie, black jogging pants, black running shoes and a pair of binoculars; of course, black. The bottom portion contains items that look more interesting.

A large black shoulder bag contains several dozen passports issued under as many different names, several dozen wads of currency from as many different countries, a wallet containing a debit card, a credit card, bank details, a Newfoundland driver's license, and a flashlight...black. Underneath the shoulder bag is another opaque plastic chest about one third the size of the original but otherwise identical.

I place the larger chest by my feet and lift the smaller chest onto my lap. Again, a digital display appears on its milky face, only this time there are fourteen zeros. I'm now operating with an increasing degree of confidence and immediately check my wristwatch. The date 2020.07.30 appears followed by 07.49.10. I turn the watch face to the reading...*transfer sequence*... and I'm just about to touch the watch face when everything suddenly becomes devastatingly clear. My predomination of pending doom, my overwhelming dread of a serious miscalculation, explained in an instant.

The year is wrong!

I had thought there was an error in the time of day when the sun had appeared misplaced in the midday sky. Then I had suspected a miscalculation in location when no land had been in sight. But now I know, the miscalculation is in the date.

Although 2020 is an important year in my past, I have returned from the year 2365 to prevent an invasion of microscopic aliens that have been programed to systematically destroy all carbon-based matter on Earth. But I've returned to the wrong time segment. I'm fifteen years too late. The silicon microbes had been introduced to Earth's inhabitants in the year 2005 and by 2020 would have already assimilated with most of the population and have already been activated. Is it still possible to save some of Earth's present-day population?

I let my mind sift through vague memories and indistinct facts as I continue trying to piece together the plan details. Is there a contingency plan? My mind drifts through the years, then decades, then centuries. I let myself go with the flow, hoping that the free flow of random thoughts would trigger complete cognizance. I need more answers.

Decisively I increase my speed and activate the fourteen-digit transfer sequence. I may not be able to save the rest of this world but there is one person I know I can save. And that makes this trip worthwhile.

CPSIA information can be obtained
at www.ICGtesting.com
Printed in the USA
LVHW040406190423
744640LV00008B/554

9 781638 292463